JOEY'S HEAD

JOEY'S HEAD

Gladys Cretan · Illustrated by Blanche Sims

HALF MOON BOOKS

Published by Simon & Schuster

New York · London · Toronto · Sydney · Tokyo · Singapore

To Aram, Jeff, and Joel,
the Cretan card collectors—G.C.

To Babe and Bernie—B.S.

HALF MOON BOOKS
Simon & Schuster Building, Rockefeller Center
1230 Avenue of the Americas, New York, New York 10020
Text copyright © 1991 by Gladys Cretan. Illustrations copyright © 1991 by Blanche Sims.
First paperback edition 1993
All rights reserved including the right of reproduction in whole or in part in any form.
HALF MOON BOOKS and Colophon are trademarks of Simon & Schuster.
Designed by Lucille Chomowicz
Also available in a SIMON & SCHUSTER BOOKS FOR YOUNG READERS hardcover edition.
Manufactured in the United States of America   10 9 8 7 6 5 4 3 2 1
Library of Congress Cataloging-in-Publication Data: Cretan, Gladys Yessayan. Joey's head /
by Gladys Cretan; illustrated by Blanche Sims. p.   cm.   Summary: Mike whips up a fake
"magic" potion to get rid of his troublesome younger brother Joey, but the potion works
and makes Joey's head disappear. [1. Brothers—Fiction.   2. Magic—Fiction.]
I. Sims, Blanche, ill.   II. Title. PZ7.C866Jo 1991 [E]—dc20   90-41592 CIP   AC
ISBN: 0-671-73201-3 (HC)   ISBN: 0-671-86699-0 (PBK)

Contents

1 Shock Waves!

Sure, I'm always saying "Get lost, Joey!" Or "Drop dead, Joey!" But I don't mean for it to really happen.

And actually he didn't drop dead. He just disappeared.

Honest, he disappeared. Today. Right in front of me. But not all of him. Just his head. The rest of him was still sitting there in his blue T-shirt, and he was talking to me in his regular little brother pesty voice. But no head.

That's what I said. No head.

I have to admit that all the way home from school I kept hoping Joey wouldn't be there for a change. But that was dumb. Where else would he be?

Mrs. Terrance was ready to leave the minute I got home, the way she always is. You can't blame her. She's been cooped up with the world's biggest mouth ever since she picked him up from morning kindergarten. Now I'm stuck for two whole hours before Mom gets home.

Joey doesn't skip a beat. He follows me right down the hall, chirping. Then I reach my bedroom. Shock waves!

2 Secret Brew

That kid has been into my baseball cards.
My prize collection. All mixed up and all
over the place. On the bed. The pillows.
The desk. Even the floor.

I'm talking about a collection from
years and years back, when my granddad
and my dad and uncle were collecting,
until now. I have Yankees and Giants
complete back to 1955. Dad says a
collection like that is worth lots of money,
but I always tell him I wouldn't sell it.

And here's Joey, all happy, saying "Look, Mike, I helped you. I put all those cards together."

"Together!" I yell. "What do you mean, together? They're all mixed up. And maybe some are even missing."

"No," he says, "I didn't lose any. And look, I put all the pitchers in one pile, and here's the pile of all the shortstops. This one looks pretty old though."

Sure old. Yogi Berra, from the 1951 Yankees, for gosh sakes. Last spring Ted Berger's big brother, who has a baseball-card store, offered to trade me the whole 1968 Dodgers lineup for that one card.

I stand there with my fists clenched. The only thing stopping me from really winging that kid is the sure feeling that if I do, Mom will come home and wing me. She seems to like him somehow.

I let out a big roar and I yell "Go lose yourself! Just disappear!"

I stomp off to the kitchen and slam the door.

The dumb kid follows me. He doesn't even know when he's in big trouble.

"Teams!" I yell at him. "Don't you know those cards were all in teams, for gosh sakes? And you've gone and messed them all up!"

"Gee," he says. "Gee, Mike."

I grab a bowl and pour in some cold cereal.

"What are you doing?" he says.

Bright kid.

"What do you think I'm doing?" I say. "I'm making a secret brew."

Don't ask me why I said that. Just cracking wise because I'm mad. But he believes me.

"Gee," he says again. He looks at the bowl all wide-eyed.

"Yeah," I say, "secret brew. From the olden days. My gang learned about it on our mystery Indian bike hike. See this brown stuff?"

I reach over and grab the soy sauce, and start pouring.

"Wow," he says, "it's brown all right." He can hardly look away from the bowl.

Now I'm hooked. I'm pounding mad, and I'm grabbing everything, and I'm pouring, and it's making me feel better. That cereal does not snap or crackle. It's all mooshed up with apple juice. I pour in a bunch of spices and then I say to Joey, "Okay, it's time for the secret ingredient. Close your eyes."

He squints his eyes tight shut. I throw in some white stuff and flaky stuff and

keep stirring and grabbing and pouring and stirring. It's all food, but it sure looks awful. Finally I run out of steam and sit at the table, breathing hard, like I just finished a race.

Joey looks from the bowl to me. "Gosh," he says, "I didn't know you knew how to do that, Mike." Then he says, "What does it do?"

"Do?" I say.

"If you drink it," he says, "what happens?"

I'm not ready for that one, so I stall. "Oh, certain mysterious things," I say. "Things the Indians understand."

"Let's drink it," he says. "Maybe we'll get to be like the Indians."

"Sure, go ahead," I say. "Try some."

The kid is fearless. He dips into the bowl with a cup and gulps the stuff down.

"How is it?" I ask.

"Terrible."

"Oh sure," I say. "That's how it is with secret brews. They usually taste bad. That's so everybody won't drink them. Only the right people."

"Was I one of the right people?" Joey asks.

Before I can figure out what to say, Joey begins to fade. Before my eyes. Fading. But not all of him. Just his head.

3 The Bag Head

"Joey?" I say. And then I yell it. "Joey!"

"What's the matter with you?" he says. "What's wrong?"

"Wrong?" I say. "You're not there, that's what's wrong."

"What do you mean?" he says. "Of course I'm here." He waves his two hands in front of him.

"Joey," I say, "honest, your head isn't there."

"You're trying to scare me," he says,

and he starts to cry. I can tell he's crying because I can hear it. But he's not there. Not his head.

"You're mad because I messed up your cards."

"Cards," I say. "What cards?"

"Anyway, I don't believe you," Joey says. "I have a head. Just like you do."

I walk him over to Mom's little mirror over the sink. I start to put my arm around his shoulder, and then I sort of pull it away. I mean, this whole thing is spooky. Joey stands on his tiptoes and looks and then screams.

"Where's my head?" he screams. "You get my head back, Mike!"

"Me?" I say. "You expect me to get your head back?"

"You know how to do the secret brew," he says. "Now do the rest. Whatever it is."

"Joey," I say, "I don't know anything else. And I'm pouring this brew down the sink right now."

"You better know," he says. His voice is shaking. "You better know the rest or you'll be in big trouble. I'll tell Mom on you."

"Listen," I say, "we need help. Before

Mom gets home. Let's get out of here. We'll go find my friends."

"Good," Joey says. "Maybe they'll remember the rest of the secret."

Then he starts to chicken out.

"I can't," he says. "I have no head. Everyone will stare at me."

"What do you care?" I say. "They won't even know who you are."

But Joey won't budge. So I put a bag over his head. That is, I put a bag where his head used to be.

"I can't see!" he says.

I take the bag off Joey and cut holes where the eyes should be, even though I feel creepy doing it, and we start out.

It's a good thing we have the bag on his so-called head because right there in the elevator we run into Mr. Everet, the apartment manager. He thinks Joey's being funny, so he makes a couple of cracks about always having said that Joey had a face only a mother could love, so it's a good idea to cover it up. I try to smile back.

We walk down the street and what a relief, most people think it's a joke. One lady says to her friend, "Look, what a great idea. I'll try that the next time I look ugly in the mirror. Maybe tomorrow morning."

"Just act natural," I say to Joey. "We're almost to the park."

"How do I act natural?" Joey says.

Good question. How does a bag-head act natural?

"Hello, gentlemen," Mr. Hajeb calls out. "Time for a piece of fruit, right?"

Trapped. My mom has a standing order with Mr. Hajeb to give us a piece of fruit any afternoon we're around his store. She pays him when she shops there on the weekend.

He hands an apple to me and one to Joey. "Taste," he says. "Wonderful." And he stands there, smiling. I take a big bite and hope Joey thinks to run off while I stall around.

"It's really good, Mr. Hajeb," I say.

"Aha! And the young mister?" he says.

"Oh, I don't think he should . . ." I start, but then I see what Joey is doing. Good for him! He pokes the apple up into the bag from the bottom, and he makes a

crunching noise. "It's good," he says in a
normal voice. Smart kid.

I say, "See you later, Mr. Hajeb. We
have to hurry right now," and we take off
fast. "That was pretty good, Joey."

"What?" he says.

"Pretending to eat the apple," I say.

"What do you mean?" he says,
and before I can answer he pulls his hand
down out of the bag and hands me an'
apple core. I jump a foot.

He says, "What's the matter?"

I say, "How did you eat the apple?"

"What's so strange about eating an apple?" he says. Then he gets that choky sound again. "See?" he says. "You really don't believe I'm here anymore."

I feel a lot better in the playground with all those kids running around and riding bikes. A kid with a bag pulled over his head doesn't look too strange in all that commotion.

Not even to my friends. When we walk up, Ann Marie says, "Hi," and Richard even says, "Hi, Joey, what's doing?"

Steve says, "How come you had to bring him?"

I say, "Listen, you all. I'm in big trouble."

4 "Is This a Trick?"

They crowd around.

"It's Joey," I say. "It's his head."

Steve says, "What's the matter with his head?"

Ann Marie says, "Is something wrong?"

"Wrong?" Joey hollers. "Can't you see something's wrong?"

"No," she says back. "How can we see when you're covered up?"

Steve reaches over to Joey's bag.

"You stop that!" Joey screams.

"What's the matter with the dumb kid?" Steve says to me.

"Well," I say, "he drank this secret brew I made. And his head disappeared."

"Oh sure!" she says. "Disappeared."

"Honest," I say. "Honest."

"That's why we came to see you," Joey says.

"We don't have your head," Steve says. Wise guy.

"The magic kid, Joey!" Richard hollers. "Come and see the boy with no head!" He grabs for Joey's bag. "Let's see the empty space!"

"Stop!" Joey yells. "You stop that!"

But Richard doesn't stop. He pulls off the bag. Then he's so surprised, that he lets go, and the bag goes flying away in the wind.

"Are you crazy?" I scream. "Look what you've done!"

No one answers. They all stand staring at Joey. Petrified.

But Joey's not petrified. He's jumping and yelling, "My bag! You get my bag back!"

"Jee-pers," Steve says. "The kid's right. Get his bag back."

Richard shakes himself loose and runs after the bag, but it's too late. Two girls on bikes have just rolled over it.

"I know! The helmet," Richard says.

"The helmet!"

Richard runs to his bike and grabs a black plastic helmet. "Here," he says to Joey. "Here!" He slaps it down where Joey's head is supposed to be. "It's my brother's motorcycle helmet," he says. "He lent it to me.

"Look," he says to the rest of us, "it even has a face guard. That is, if he had a face."

"I have a face!" Joey says.

"Well, where is it?" Richard yells.

"I don't know," Joey says.

"You two are in real trouble," Steve says. "I think you need a doctor."

"When I sprained my ankle," Ann Marie says, "my dad took me to Dr. Spender. Over in that big medical building. A missing head is worse than a sprained ankle."

Joey isn't that easy to deal with.

"Why do I have to go to a doctor?" he says. "He's not the one who knows about secret powers."

"Look," I say, "some things need a doctor, and this might be one of them. We'd better hurry because Mom will be home soon."

At the doctor's the kids sit in a row across the room. When the nurse opens a little window and peeks out from her office and says "Is there a problem?" they all point at Joey. Ann Marie says, "It's his head."

The nurse says, "What happened to it?"

Joey says, "I don't know!" and he starts to cry and grabs my arm.

She opens a door and says, "Why don't you two come back here."

"Okay," I say, "but we need a doctor right away."

"First things first," she says cheerfully. "Do you have insurance?"

"Insurance?" I say. "Listen, we have a terrible problem. Where's the doctor?"

"An emergency?" she says. "Why didn't you tell me? Let's see that head," and the nurse reaches for Joey's helmet.

"No!" I yell. "Wait!"

The doctor comes out of a side room and heads over to us. "Did I hear there's an emergency?"

"You bet!" I say. "A genuine terrible emergency."

"It's my head!" Joey says.

"What happened to it?" the doctor says, reaching for the helmet.

"It's gone," I tell him.

He puts his hand back down.

"Gone? What does that mean?"

"Honest," I say. "It plain disappeared."

"Is this a trick?" he says. "I have sick people to take care of inside. I don't have time for games." He stomps off.

The nurse says, "Would you like me to call your parents to pick you up?"

"Parents?" I yell. "C'mon, Joey!"

I grab his hand, and we dash out with the other kids close behind.

All I can think of is to head for home, fast, and hide Joey. Somehow.

"See you tomorrow," I say to the others.

They say "Right" and "Hasta mañana" and "Ciao" and "See you" the way they always do, but they don't sound too sure of really seeing us again. I can tell.

5 What a Mess!

When we finally get home Joey runs to
the kitchen and says, "Okay, let's try.
Really try. Otherwise I'll tell on you, and
you'll be in big trouble."

"Honest, Joey," I say, "about those
secret powers—" then I stop because I
hear that old familiar sound, the front
door opening. Jeepers.

"Hi, you two," Mom says. "I'm home!"

I hear her hanging her coat in the closet
and I say to Joey, "Quick. Get under the
table."

"No way," Joey says.

"Come on!" I say.

"Not unless you're doing the secret stuff!" he says.

"Hide, Joey!" I beg him.

"So start," he says quietly.

"Okay," I say quickly. "Okay."

I grab a bowl and start pouring stuff into it. Soy sauce. Cereal. Ketchup. Good so far. Apple juice, arrowroot powder, what else? Root beer? Peanut butter. Right. Black stuff. White stuff. Grainy stuff. Fast. Tea leaves. Oh gosh. What if I

change the recipe? Or does it even matter? Marmalade? I'm reaching and pouring and I'm feeling pretty weird.

I give Joey a cup of the new brew.

He says, "I knew you could do it."

This time I actually put my arm around his shoulder. "C'mon, Joey," I say. "Don't you know I really want to help you?

Don't you know I really, sort of, uh, like you? Honest!"

"Honest?" he says.

"Yes, honest!" I say. "And now move! Hide!" I shove him all the way under the table.

"Hi," Mom says, "and where's your favorite brother?"

"Hiding," I say. "It's a game."

"Sure is a messy game," she says. "What a shambles."

She washes a pear and bites into it. "Delicious," she says. "Don't you want one? It's a while before dinner."

"No thanks, Mom," I say. "We aren't hungry."

"Speak for yourself," she says. "What about you under there, Joey? You're always hungry."

She's seen him. I'm sunk.

"Um, no thanks," Joey says from down under. "Mr. Hajeb gave us apples."

"Gosh, Mom," I say, "you're sort of spoiling the game. You're not supposed to be able to see him yet."

"Sorry," she says, "I wouldn't want to spoil a game. Next time," she says, talking down to Joey, "you better hide more carefully. The way you're spread out I can see your sneakers sticking out at this end, and your hair at the other."

She walks off, humming. Hair? Did she say hair?

I hear Joey scuffling out from under the table. I hold my breath and turn slowly to look at him. And I let out a scream!

"Hey!" Joey says. "Aren't you glad my head's back?"

"But it's not!" I yell. "It's not!"

"It is too," he says. "Mom said so!"

"She said she saw your hair," I yell. "And that's all there is. Your hair. All by itself!"

"No problem," he says, "now that we know what to do about it."

I can't believe this. He scrambles back under the table.

"Boy," he says, "you did that just in time."

"Did what?" I ask.

"Made the brew," he says. "Stay cool. I'll drink some more." I hear him gulping.

"It still tastes awful," he says. "Take another look."

I kneel down, look under the table, and let out another screech.

"What?" Joey says. "What?"

"One ear!" I say. "Now you have hair and one ear. Ohmygosh!"

"Gee, Mike, stop worrying!" he says.

Sure. Why worry?

I am zombied out. I'm sitting on the floor, holding my head, rocking back and forth.

"Gosh," Joey says. "Is that what you have to do? Rock in a trance? Do you have to say any secret words to yourself?"

"What are you talking about?" I say. "What secret words?"

"How would I know?" he says. "Okay, now look at me again."

I hold my breath and turn. He smiles. With his mouth. And his eyes. His eyes in his face. In his head. I see his whole head! I have never seen anything so wonderful in my whole life.

"I always knew you could get my head back," he says, grinning.

But all I can say is, "I'd better clean up this mess now."

He grabs the helmet and heads down the hall to watch TV, just like any old time. He's happy.

He turns back and says, "Hey, Mike, do you want me to help you straighten out your baseball cards?"

"Baseball cards?" I holler at him. "Are you nuts? Not on your life! And you better leave those cards alone, or I'll . . ." Then I stop. I better be careful.

Remember how this whole thing started?

About the author

Gladys Yessayan Cretan is the author of many books for children, including *All Except Sammy*, *Lobo and Brewster*, and *Sunday for Sona*.

Ms. Cretan grew up in the San Francisco Bay Area, now lives in San Mateo, California, and is pleased that her grown children also live on that peninsula. Although her sons keep asking her what she has done with their old baseball card collection, she insists she never touched it.

About the illustrator

Blanche Sims has illustrated the Kids of the Polk Street School books by Patricia Reilly Giff, *I Took My Frog to the Library* by Eric A. Kimmell, and many others. She lives in Westport, Connecticut.